SOO LING
FINDS A WAY

JUNE BEHRENS

Pictures by

TARO YASHIMA

GOLDEN GATE JUNIOR BOOKS
San Carlos, California

For Hank, Teri and Denise

Soo Ling stood in front of Grandfather Soo's Golden Lotus Hand Laundry.
She watched the men at work on the new building across the street.

"What kind of a store do you suppose it will be, Ting-a-ling?" she asked her kitten. "Will there be toys, or candy and ice cream?"

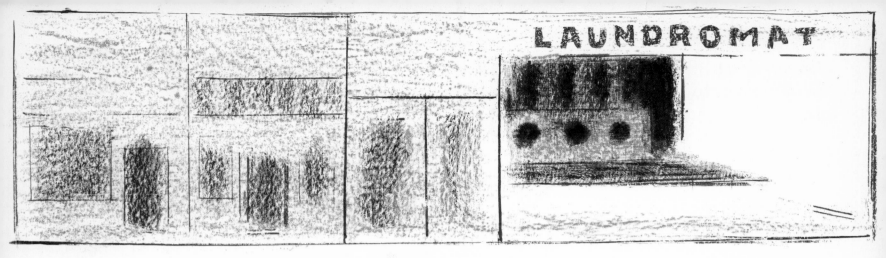

Soo Ling couldn't believe her eyes when she read the sign on the new store the next day. "LAUNDROMAT," she spelled.

"Come along, Ting-a-ling," she said.
"We'll have to tell Grandfather Soo
about this."

For a long minute Soo Ling watched Grandfather Soo and his iron at work. *Zip . . . Tip . . . Flip. Swish, Swosh, Swish.*
Grandfather Soo worked as fast as a magic-maker. But today the busy iron did not bring a smile to Soo Ling's face.

Grandfather Soo looked down into sad eyes. "What troubles my little
Soo Ling?" he asked.

60
WASHERS
15 DRIERS

LAUNDROMAT   OPEN 6AM-11PM

Soo Ling pointed to the bright new sign
across the street. "Just look at that,
Grandfather," she said.

Grandfather Soo stared at the letters on the sign. "It is the new way, my child," he said. "We may have to close the Golden Lotus Hand Laundry."

He shut the door and went back to his work.

Soo Ling sat on the doorstep. She
wanted to cry. "Ting-a-ling, there
must be some way to help Grandfather
Soo," she said.

Mr. Jun, the postman, looked down at little Soo Ling. "Where is Miss Sunshine today?" he asked.

"Look across the street," said Soo Ling. "What will happen to our Golden Lotus Hand Laundry now?"

"The machines will never do the work
of your Grandfather Soo," said Mr.
Jun. "Now let me see a happy smile."

The mothers at the grocery store talked of nothing but the new laundromat. But Mr. Sing, the grocer, called to Soo Ling, "Tell Grandfather I will bring him my aprons tomorrow. The new machines will wash, but someone must iron the clothes. No machine can work the magic of your grandfather's iron."

Soo Ling was smiling as she carried home the cabbage and peas she had come to buy.

On the day the laundromat opened for business people came from here,
from there, from everywhere.

Soo Ling sat and watched them come
with their big bundles of laundry.
"Those people have never even seen
Grandfather Soo make his iron work
like magic," she said to her kitten.

Suddenly she had an idea. She jumped
up and ran into the Golden Lotus
Hand Laundry with Ting-a-ling at
her heels.

Soo Ling pulled her grandfather over to the front window. "The people will see you and your magic iron if you stand here and work, Grandfather," she said.

Grandfather Soo said nothing, but he moved his work to the window to make Soo Ling happy.

A few people stood and watched Grandfather Soo at work. A mother waved. The policeman stopped for a moment to gaze. Little noses were pressed against the window. The magic of Grandfather's busy iron brought wonder to the faces at the window.

Zip . . . Tip . . . Flip! Swish, Swosh, Swish!

A big man with no hair watched Grandfather Soo for a long time. Then
he went into the Golden Lotus Hand Laundry.

"I am Mr. Lee," he said. "Will you move across the street to my new laundromat? My machines will wash the clothes. You can iron them. I will make you my partner." Grandfather Soo was pleased. "I will come," he said. "I will be part of the new way."

"Yippeee!" shouted Soo Ling, who had been listening in the doorway.

On the day of the Grand Opening of the laundromat Grandfather Soo worked proudly in the window.

The *Zip . . . Tip . . . Flip* and the
Swish, Swosh, Swish of his iron
brought many smiles.

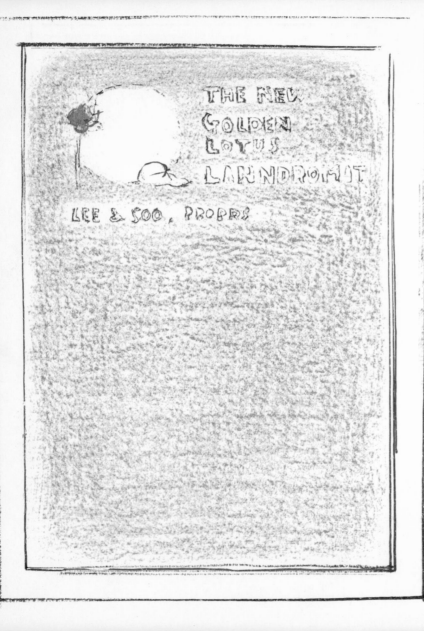

Soo Ling's smile was bigger than a bright new moon as she read the sign on the window —

THE NEW

GOLDEN LOTUS

LAUNDROMAT

LEE AND SOO, PROPRS.

SOO LING FINDS A WAY

JUNE BEHRENS
Pictures by TARO YASHIMA

Little Soo Ling had watched the new building going up across the street from Grandfather Soo's Golden Lotus Hand Laundry with interest, but when she read the sign, LAUNDROMAT, above the door her heart was filled with dismay. To be sure, Grandfather Soo could wield his iron faster than anyone in the world, but would modern competition prove too strong, tempting his customers to forsake the old way for the new? Grandfather thought that it would and feared that the Golden Lotus Hand Laundry must soon close its doors forever. Then Soo Ling had an inspiration, one that not only brought a joyful solution to Grandfather's problem but gave the utmost satisfaction to everyone in the neighborhood.